BATMAN™ vs. THE JOKER

Written by Julia March

CONTENTS

YOU'LL NEVER BEAT US, JOKER!

BRING IT ON, BATMAN!

CHAPTER 1: VEHICLES

Vehicles are not just for getting from A to B! Cars, bikes, helicopters, and more all play a part in the high-speed, high-stakes battle between good and evil.

BATMAN vs. THE JOKER

Batman and the Joker go head-to-head in their vehicles. The Batwing is fast, but the Joker's ice cream truck is packed with wacky weapons!

When Batman needs to fight crime, he hops into one of his many amazing vehicles! He is ready for anything.

My speedy **BATWING** will leave you in the dust!

YOU'RE TOO SLOW— AND THAT'S NO JOKE!

Bat-symbol designs make my ride look **SO COOL**

Batman's Batwing vehicle

The Joker's ice cream truck

I'll blast you with my **HILARIOUS ICE CREAM CANNON**

This **LAUGHING GAS POPSICLE** will leave you with a smile on your face!

DID YOU KNOW?

The ice cream truck's trunk can store extra weapons. Sometimes the Joker fills it with his favorite—laughing gas!

Even my truck **CAN'T STOP SMILING!**

Which vehicle would you like to drive?

 OR

NIGHTWING VS. HARLEY QUINN

The race is on! Nightwing's car is faster than Harley Quinn's, but Harley has plenty of sneaky tricks on board. Will speed or sneakiness win?

I'll use this baton to JAM YOUR WHEELS

STOP CLOWNING AROUND, HARLEY!

Your tricks won't help you if you CAN'T CATCH ME!

Don't try throwing anything sharp, my tires are PUNCTURE RESISTANT!

Nightwing's car

Harley's car goes forward, backward, and in circles! It doesn't need fuel—but Harley has to stop to wind it up now and then!

My huge **MALLET** will dent your little car!

Harley Quinn's wind-up car

DID YOU KNOW?

Harley's colorful costume is based on the suit of a medieval jester. She dyes her hair half red, half blue to match!

My car is full of **TRICK WEAPONS!**

Who will be king or queen of the road?

OR

I'll fire this **GRAPPLING HOOK** and latch onto your Catmobile!

THIS ROBIN IS TOO FLY FOR YOU!

DID YOU KNOW?

After stealing diamonds, Catwoman often steals a carton of milk, too. Crime is thirsty work! Batman is returning this one to the supermarket.

Robin's car

ROBIN VS. CATWOMAN

Catwoman has been on a crime spree! Robin is chasing the Catmobile in his car. Can he catch the cat and send her home empty-clawed?

Robin stands up to drive his car. Well, he only has short legs! His initial, "R," is on the rear spoiler to deter anyone who might try to steal it.

My **BIG BIKE** will turn your car into crushed ice!

DID YOU KNOW?

Batman's bike has three wheels. It's narrow at the back but very wide at the front—ideal for ramming villains off the road.

Batman's bike

MUFFLERS make my bike smooth and quiet, just like me!

BATMAN VS. KILLER FROST

Batman is fighting to keep Killer Frost out of Gotham City. If she gets in, she will suck the heat out of the city and power up for a chilling crime spree!

Killer Frost absorbs heat from enemies and converts it into cold. She then uses it to make icy weapons and missiles!

THIS ISN'T A VERY WARM WELCOME!

You can't keep me out! My ice car is **A BULLDOZER** and it can smash through anything!

Killer Frost's Ice Car

Gray is boring ... this year's color is **ICE BLUE!**

Who will win this hotly contested battle?

WONDER WOMAN VS. DOOMSDAY

Doomsday is destroying everything he sees. But here comes Wonder Woman in her Invisible Jet. Doomsday might soon meet his own doom!

Foes don't see the Invisible Jet coming! Wonder Woman steers it with her mind, so her hands are free to use a sword.

Look sharp! This sword can **CHOP UP ATOMS!**

My jet can become totally invisible. It's **CLEARLY THE BEST!**

Invisible Jet

LOOK OUT FOR MY POISON POWER!

My costume is tipped with **POISON!** Hey ... want a hug?

DID YOU KNOW?

Doomsday evolved on the planet Krypton. Unlike humans, he does not need to eat, sleep, or even breathe!

My car is protected by **JAGGED BONES**

Doomsday's car

Which one will make their enemy disappear?

A **OR**

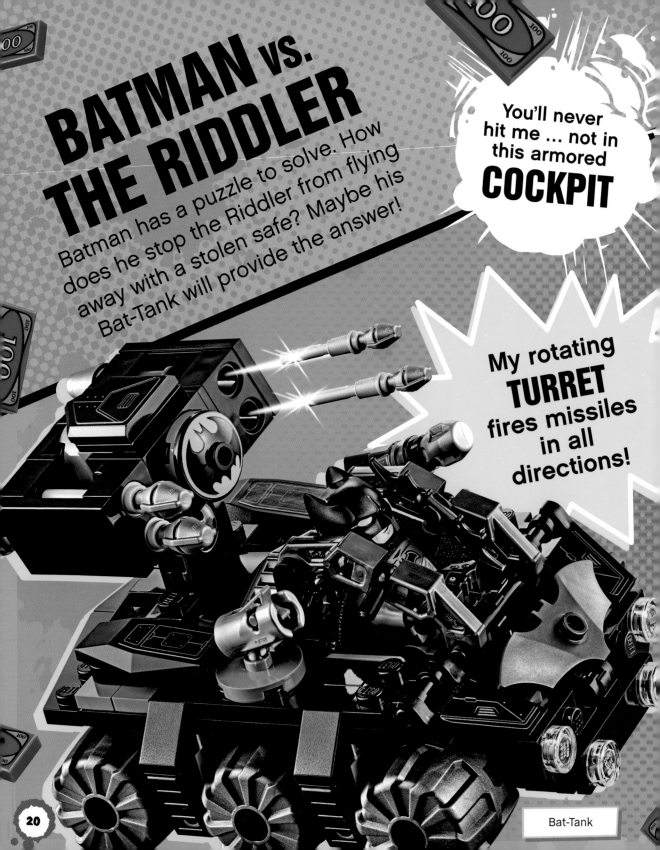

BATMAN vs. THE RIDDLER

Batman has a puzzle to solve. How does he stop the Riddler from flying away with a stolen safe? Maybe his Bat-Tank will provide the answer!

You'll never hit me ... not in this armored **COCKPIT**

My rotating **TURRET** fires missiles in all directions!

Bat-Tank

The Riddler landed his helicopter on the bank's roof. He then used the anchor and chain to hook a safe full of valuables!

Can you dodge the spinning shooters on **MY ROTOR?**

WHAT'S GREEN AND CAN FLY?

The Riddler's helicopter

DID YOU KNOW?

To open a safe, you must turn the dial to the correct numbers. The cunning crook easily cracks the code to this one!

First the heist, now the **HOIST!**

Which one will get the safe?

OR

DID YOU KNOW?

The Batsub has two detachable tail fins. If Batman has to abandon sub, he fixes the fins to his feet and swims away.

Batsub

TWO ENGINES

give twice the power ... simple math!

I CAN BREATHE EASILY IN MY BUBBLE COCKPIT

Come here ... I'll grab you with these adjustable

CLAWS

BATMAN VS. BLACK MANTA

Black Manta is cruising the ocean in his submarine, looking for treasure to steal! Luckily, Batman is ready for him in a fin-tastic new sub of his own.

Black Manta's sub looks like a stingray, with wings and a tail. But unlike a ray—or any other fish—it boasts an array of shooters.

My Manta Sub looks **VERY FISHY**

GRR! I'LL BURST YOUR BUBBLE!

MY SHOOTER will blast your propellers off!

Black Manta's submarine

Whose sub will end up ruling the waves?

 OR

SUPERMAN VS. BIZARRO

Bizarro is a backward version of Superman who wants to turn the world upside down. Can Superman put Bizarro's plans into reverse?

Superman has heat vision and freeze breath. That's the exact opposite of Bizarro's ice vision and flame breath!

Just call me the **MAN OF WHEEL!**

STOP YOUR BACK TALK, BIZARRO!

GIANT FISTS on my car pack a punch!

Superman's car

Me am turning Superman into weakling with green **KRYPTONITE**

DID YOU KNOW?

Kryptonite is a special crystal. Green Kryptonite weakens Superman, but for Bizarro, only the blue form is dangerous.

Bizarro's back-to-front car

Me hit brakes to **GO FASTER.** Boom!

Who will succeed in driving their enemy away?

BATMAN VS. MR. FREEZE

What's that chill in the air? Mr. Freeze is zooming into town on his snow scooter, and he wants to freeze Batman! Things are about to heat up ...

The Batmobile has flaming exhausts. If it gets too close, it could put the snow scooter into meltdown!

You'll never be as **COOL** as me!

I'LL TURN YOUR PLANS TO SLUSH

How do you like my bat wing **TAIL FINS?**

Batmobile

Mr. Freeze's snow scooter

My red thermal **GOGGLES** scan for targets ... like you!

DID YOU KNOW?

Mr. Freeze is an expert in ice-cold technology. His favorite weapon is a twin-barreled freeze gun that turns enemies to ice.

What could be cooler than a motorcycle **ON SKIS?**

Who will win this battle of heat vs. cold?

DID YOU KNOW?

Batman has made a promise never to use guns. Instead, he throws bat-shaped weapons called Batarangs at his enemies.

HERE I COME IN MY JET-POWERED BAT-GLIDER ...

I am a master of all the **MARTIAL ARTS** in the world. Beat that!

My **UTILITY BELT** is loaded with cool gadgets

BATMAN VS. LEX LUTHOR

Batman and Lex Luthor have no superpowers, so they rely on gadgets and skill. Who will win their air battle, and who will crash and burn?

Lex Luthor is a powerful businessman who can't stand Super Heroes. He's always trying to chase them out of Metropolis.

UP, UP, AND AWAY IN MY ESCAPE POD!

Check out my **BATTLE SUIT** with its energy shield!

I'll use the **FOLD-OUT WINGS** to change speed and direction

Lex Luthor

Who will be the last man flying?

 OR

Wheel opens the Fear Gas tank

Scarecrow sits up in the cockpit

Scarecrow's **GAS GUN** fires Fear Gas missiles at victims. Bull's-eye!

Fear Gas is released from the tank through this tube

HOW DO YOU LIKE OUR HA-HA HARVESTER?

ROTATING BLADES chop up anything in the harvester's path— not just corn!

DID YOU KNOW?

The harvester's gas tank holds Fear Gas, ready to fire at victims! It is also big enough to trap the farmer inside!

HARVEST OF FEAR

It's countryside chaos! The Joker and Scarecrow are menacing a poor farmer in their crazy harvester. Drive, farmer, drive ...

NOOO ... DON'T MOW ME DOWN!

This big-wheeled red tractor is not a good getaway vehicle. It's built for hauling heavy farm equipment, not for speed.

Tractor's exhaust pipe

THE FLASH VS. CAPTAIN COLD

Captain Cold hopes to push The Flash off the road, freeze him, and pelt him with snow cones! Can The Flash disarm him in time?

The Flash is often attacked by a team of super-villains called the Rogues. The team is led by The Flash's archenemy, Captain Cold!

The Flash's car

YOU'RE ON THIN ICE, CAPTAIN COLD!

The flames from my **EXHAUST** will melt your weapons

SPEED LIMIT? This car doesn't have one!

I feel so cool in my
ICE-BLUE PARKA
and snow visor

THIS SHOULD BE A PUSHOVER!

DID YOU KNOW?

Captain Cold's gun freezes people's atoms so they can't move. He once froze a whole city in its tracks!

I'll shove you aside with my **SNOWPLOW**

Captain Cold's snowplow

Who will win? The speedster or the freezer?

 OR

BATWOMAN VS. BROTHER EYE

Brother Eye is a satellite gone rogue. It spreads a virus that turns people into scary cyber-soldiers! Can Batwoman knock it out of the sky?

There's no doubt who owns this craft! It has bat wings, shooters, and places to attach bat weapons and elements.

I'll make you STOP STARING!

Ready, aim ...
BULL'S-EYE!

Batjet

I'LL FINISH YOU IN THE BLINK OF AN EYE!

Even my STEERING wheel is bat-shaped!

I'll befuddle you with **EYE-POPPING** energy beams!

Brother Eye

Come closer ... my **TALONS AWAIT!**

OR

BATMAN VS. KILLER MOTH

Killer Moth is buzzing in to face off with Batman. The Dark Knight is coming right back at him in his flame-red Batcopter. The fight is on!

Beware, moths! Batman's flame-red Batcopter has wings and a rotor. The cockpit gives Batman a great view for aiming Batarangs!

Batcopter

My boosters will **PROPEL** me way out of reach!

STOP BUGGING ME, MOTH!

The windshield protects me while I aim **BATARANGS** at you!

36

I'll squirt you with goo from my **COCOON GUN**

My agile flyer can **FLY CIRCLES AROUND YOU**

DID YOU KNOW?

Killer Moth's flyer looks like a big bug. It has a stinger in the tail and a gun in the nose that sprays sleeping gas at enemies!

My flyer's wings will **SWAT** your Batarang away!

Killer Moth's flyer

Which one will bring his foe crashing down?

 OR

BATMAN VS. HARLEY QUINN

Batman's out on his Batcycle, but someone's chasing him! It's Harley Quinn, and she wants to race. Can her bike really beat Batman's?

The Batcycle is designed to be bulletproof ... but it has never been tested against giant mallet attacks! Will it hold up?

Batman's Batcycle

I'LL HIT TOP SPEED BEFORE YOU HIT ME!

BAT BLACK is way cooler than clownish red and blue!

My bike's **STUD SHOOTERS** will knock you off course!

You'll flip when my flip-out **MALLET** bops you!

YOU'RE DRIVING ME BATTY!

Harley Quinn's bike

DID YOU KNOW?

Harley is small but strong. Her favorite weapon is a giant mallet that's almost as big as she is!

That's not me squealing ... it's my **GIANT TIRES!**

I'm a **BIG WHEEL** in the world of crime, don't you know ...

Who will win the race into Gotham City?

OR

Batcopter

HOLD TIGHT, LOIS!

This is the best copter around ... I borrowed it from BATMAN!

I've got a Robin's-eye view in this COCKPIT

ROBIN VS. LEX LUTHOR

Lex Luthor has scooped up Lois Lane with his LexCorp helicopter. He's ready for a battle with Superman ... but that's not Superman on his tail!

Robin's red Batcopter has a few planelike features. As well as a rotor on top, it has bat wings at the sides and a rear propeller.

MY ROTOR
is bigger than yours!

OH, FLY AWAY, ROBIN!

LexCorp helicopter

Grrr ... I primed my **KRYPTONITE** shooters ready for Superman!

HEY ... THIS IS FUN!

Whose helicopter rules the sky?

OR

BATMAN VS. BANE

There's a driller on the road! It's big, bad Bane trying to prove he's stronger than Batman. But Batman just won't give way. It's driving Bane crazy!

Bane believes Batman is the toughest Super Hero of all. He has become obsessed with beating the Dark Knight!

Your drill is just **BORING!**

Batmobile

GO READ THE BATWAY CODE!

DID YOU KNOW?

Batman has lots of other Batmobiles. This one has a huge engine, bat wing tail fins, and bat-symbols on the hubcaps.

My Batmobile is scratchproof, crushproof, and **DRILLPROOF!**

Bane's driller

RED HOOD VS. HARLEY

Red Hood is a very determined member of the Bat-Family. Maybe he's the one to stop Harley Quinn and her not-so-funny criminal capers!

Red Hood never takes his hood off in public. It hides the scars he got in an attack by the Joker, Harley Quinn's partner in crime.

CRIME MAKES ME SEE RED!

MY FAST **MOTORCYCLE** can catch up to any crook!

Check out the cool **SYMBOL** on my motorcycle

Red Hood

CHAPTER 2: GOTHAM CITY

Gotham City is home to Batman and his allies. It's home to the Joker and his pesky pals, too. Not to mention it's a popular hangout for visiting villains!

I am a master of 14 different styles of **HAND-TO-HAND COMBAT**

Batwoman

My high-flying **GYMNASTICS** skills give me the edge in battle!

BATWOMAN vs. THE RIDDLER

The Riddler has all kinds of tricks up his bright green sleeves. Is he a match for Batwoman's martial arts skills and high-tech gadgets?

Kate Kane is a master of stealth! She can sneak up on people undetected— very handy for catching crooks!

GENIUS LEVEL
INTELLIGENCE

DID YOU KNOW?

The Riddler uses dynamite to break into banks. His cane doubles as a crowbar for prying open safes. His skateboard helps him make a speedy getaway!

IT'S A QUESTION OF SPEED!

You will never solve my **RIDDLES AND PUZZLES!**

My cane can give you a nasty **ELECTRIC SHOCK**

The Riddler

100   100
100
100   100

Which character do you think is the coolest?

Time to fire my **NET LAUNCHER** Five, four, three ...

DID YOU KNOW?

Batman's mech is loaded with weapons. Some of them are hidden beneath bat-shaped details, like the shoulder epaulets.

I'LL SQUASH YOU FLAT, SOFTY!

Batman's mech

How about I reshape you with my **SPINNING SAW BLADE?**

50

BATMAN VS. CLAYFACE

Batman's mech is hard to beat, but Clayface is no soft touch. When mech meets mud man, one of them will come to a sticky end. But which?

Clayface is a versatile villain. He can reshape his clay body into anything he wants—even another person. Shifty!

Clayface

I'LL STICK IT TO YOU, BATMAN!

My mitts of mud will **CLOG UP** your mech!

You can't pin me down—I'm too **SLIPPERY**

Who will triumph in this battle of opposites?

 OR

The Joker does not like the orange prison suit he has to wear in Arkham Asylum. It clashes with his green hair!

One whiff of my **LAUGHING GAS** will have you rolling on the floor!

I'll shout jokes through this **MEGAPHONE** to drown out the sirens

The Joker

YOU GET IN THE CELL! I'M TAKING OVER!

DID YOU KNOW?

To let everyone know he's on the loose, the Joker takes over the prison's TV system. There's only one channel: the Joker Channel!

Who will take control of Arkham Asylum?

OR

Your **TOXINS** have no effect on me!

Batman

HEY ... ARE YOU LOSING A LEAF, IVY?

Don't bother tying me up in vines ... I'm an expert at **ESCAPING**

BATMAN vs. POISON IVY

Poison Ivy is attacking Gotham City in her plantlike mech, spreading seeds and pollen. Batman must stop her, or the city will become a jungle!

Poison Ivy uses her toxic touch to take over people's minds. Batman can resist her toxins because he is incredibly strong-minded.

54

I'll plant a **POISON KISS** on you!

NO ... I'M GRABBING THAT BATARANG!

Poison Ivy's mech

DID YOU KNOW?

Poison Ivy wants plants to take over the world! She controls plants with her mind and carries a leafy shooter.

A lash from my vine will make you break out in **ITCHY HIVES!**

Who will be the victor in this city squabble?

OR

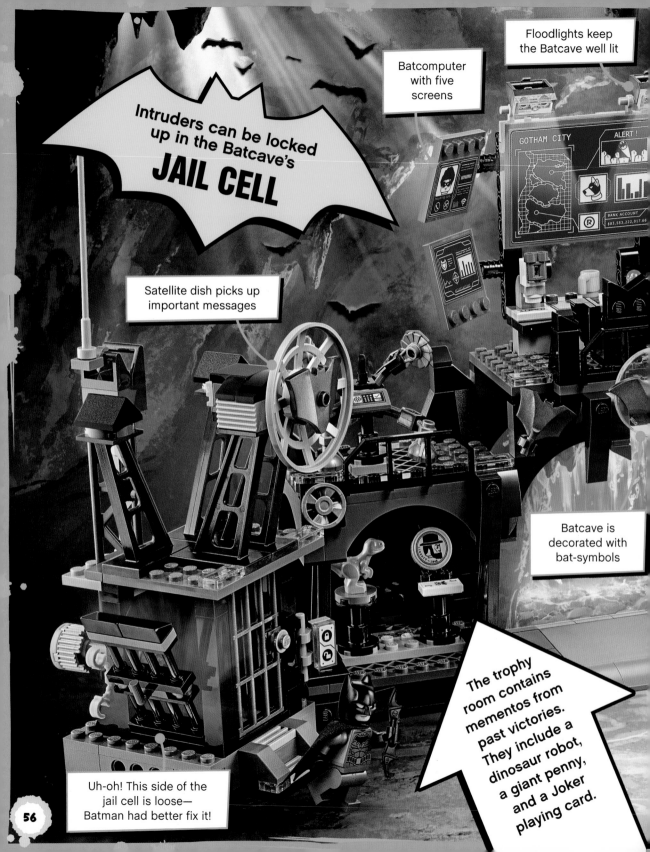

Floodlights keep the Batcave well lit

Batcomputer with five screens

Intruders can be locked up in the Batcave's **JAIL CELL**

GOTHAM CITY   ALERT!

BANK ACCOUNT
$83,553,222,017.66

Satellite dish picks up important messages

Batcave is decorated with bat-symbols

The trophy room contains mementos from past victories. They include a dinosaur robot, a giant penny, and a Joker playing card.

Uh-oh! This side of the jail cell is loose—Batman had better fix it!

Batman enters the Batcave through this hatch

The Batman Transformation **TOWER** leads down into the Batcave

DID YOU KNOW?

All the Bat-Family make regular use of the Batcave's workout zone. Super Heroes need to stay in top condition!

Grappling hooks and gas-pellet guns fill the **WEAPONS ROOM**

THE BATCAVE

Deep below Wayne Manor is Batman's secret headquarters ... the Batcave! This amazing place includes a Batcomputer zone, a trophy room, a weapons room, a workout room, and much more.

RED HOOD VS. CAPTAIN BOOMERANG

Red Hood is the angriest member of the Bat-Family. He believes in being tough on crime. That could be bad news for Captain Boomerang!

Mysterious Red Hood keeps his face hidden. His real name is Jason Todd, and he once acted as Batman's sidekick, Robin!

I'M SEEING RED, LOSERANG!

TWO BLASTERS double my chances of winning!

Batman says I'm **TOO ROUGH,** but I don't care!

Red Hood

BATMAN VS. TWO-FACE

Two-Face is double trouble. He has a half-scarred face and a dual personality. Batman needs to stop this bank robber—on the double.

I'M DYNAMITE AT PUTTING OUT EXPLOSIVES.

Batman

Aha! I used my world-famous **DETECTIVE** skills to track you down!

I'll never stop defending **GOTHAM CITY** —that's a promise

When he has a choice of doing good things or bad things, Two-Face flips his "lucky" coin to decide.

I'm not afraid of the law—I'm an **EX-LAWYER**

I'LL BEAT YOU, NO TWO WAYS ABOUT IT!

DID YOU KNOW?

Two-Face is one of Gotham City's greatest criminal crack shots. If he can't blast his way into a bank, he can usually shoot the locks off.

Two-Face

Who will win in the battle of the bank?

BATMAN VS. RĀ'S AL GHŪL

Rā's al Ghūl is in his hideout, creating a virus to attack humans. Batman can stop the villain's evil plan, but only if he beats him in an epic duel.

Rā's al Ghūl respects Batman so much, he often tries to win him over to evil. Batman always says NO!

Ha ... I found you! No wonder they call me **THE DETECTIVE**

My special **DESERT** suit is ideal for this sandy hideout.

Batman

What if I reveal your true identity, **MR. WAYNE?**

FEELING SHARP, BATMAN?

DID YOU KNOW?

Rā's al Ghūl has no fear of aging. He has control of the Lazarus Pits. These goo-filled baths restore old or sick people to youth and health.

I DETEST HUMANS ... they are ruining the Earth!

I've got more than **450 YEARS** of experience as a master swordsman!

Rā's al Ghūl

Which swordsman will prove his mettle?

OR

I'll knock the stuffing out of you with a **KARATE CHOP**

Batman

My trusty **GAS MASK** is filtering out your toxic gas

STAND DOWN, SACKHEAD!

BATMAN VS. SCARECROW

Scarecrow is aiming his Fear Gas gun at Batman, but Batman is wearing a gas mask! Maybe only hand-to-hand combat can settle this fight.

Batman's mask protects his lungs from the Scarecrow's Fear Gas. A green visor under his cowl keeps the gas out of his eyes.

I'll fire **FEAR GAS** to scare you away!

DID YOU KNOW?

Scarecrow drives a horrible harvester. Its tank holds enough Fear Gas to scare everyone for miles around!

Like my **SCARY GRIN?** I stitched it myself!

Get back—my **PITCHFORK** has pointy tines!

Scarecrow

Who will win, the Batman or the straw man?

OR

BATMAN VS. THE JOKER

Oh no! Batman has caught the Joker in the Batcave planting explosives. The Batcave and all its precious equipment could soon be blown sky high!

Batman has a wardrobe full of Batsuits. Most of them are tasteful shades of blue and gray—perfect for keeping a low profile.

No flashy colors for me! Deep blue is **MUCH CLASSIER!**

WHY THE PINK SUIT, JOKER?

Aha, caught you! I saw you on the screen of the **BATCOMPUTER!**

Batman

68

MY POISON can harm you ... **but not me!**

DID YOU KNOW?

The Joker loves comedy weapons like squirting flowers, but he also uses dynamite. His crimes are truly a blast!

I THOUGHT YOU'D BE TICKLED PINK TO SEE ME!

I'll catch this **BATARANG,** no sweat!

The Joker

Who will win the battle of the Batcave?

OR

CHAPTER 3: WIDER WORLD

Crime does not only happen in Gotham City. Wherever you go, there are super-villains ready to try their luck—and Super Heroes ready to stop them!

GREEN LANTERN VS. LEX LUTHOR

Is that Superman? The suit is right, but the face belongs to ... Lex Luthor! Is he up to no good? Maybe Green Lantern can zap a confession out of him.

Jessica Cruz uses a special power ring to make weapons out of light. She was trained by Hal Jordan, the first ever Green Lantern.

COME ON, LEX ... CONFESS!

I wear the Green Lantern Corps **SYMBOL** on my chest

Green Lantern

I'm not nervous ... I know how to **CONQUER MY FEARS!**

DID YOU KNOW?

Aquaman can communicate with sea animals. When he brings his snapping shark friend to the battle, it's crunch time for Ocean Master!

Ha! Your HELMET just looks silly ...

Only the **TRUE KING** of Atlantis can use this gold trident!

Aquaman

Face it—my **WATER JETS** are stronger than yours!

AQUAMAN VS. OCEAN MASTER

Aquaman and Ocean Master are battling beneath the waves. Which of them will win the throne of Atlantis? Tridents at the ready ...

Aquaman's trident controls the sea, and Ocean Master's trident controls lightning. It's a close contest!

Ocean Master

I'm a style icon in my bright **CAPE**

IT'S A MAGIC CROWN, AND IT CREATES CYCLONES!

Your trident can't hurt me ... I'm wearing my **ATLANTEAN ARMOR**

Who would you like to see as King of Atlantis?

OR

IF I THROW MY TIARA, YOU'LL SEE STARS!

Wonder Woman

Got you ... with my magi LASSO!

My lasso will make you CONFESS to all your crimes!

WONDER WOMAN VS. THE CHEETAH

The Cheetah is racing to attack Wonder Woman. Yikes ... she's fast! Can the Amazon princess capture the fast felon before she swipes her tiara?

Wonder Woman's royal tiara is like a boomerang ... it always returns to her. It might not stay in The Cheetah's claws for long!

So what if I get hurt? I have rapid **HEALING** powers!

When I whirl my arms, I create **CYCLONES** that put crooks in a spin!

The Flash

DID YOU KNOW?

This Blue Energy Infuser holds energy that can greatly enhance strength. Reverse-Flash didn't miss his chance to steal it!

You're fast ... but **NOT FASTER** than me!

THE FLASH VS. REVERSE-FLASH

The Flash and Reverse-Flash can run at speeds faster than light. When they go by, all you see is a blur.

The Flash taps into the Speed Force to fight crime. Reverse-Flash taps into the negative Speed Force to commit crime. No wonder they are enemies!

I can focus electricity to make my eyes **GLOW RED!** Scary, huh?

I was born in the **25TH CENTURY** and ran back through time to get here.

Reverse-Flash

Which Flash will outrun his archenemy?

 OR

SUPERMAN VS. LEX LUTHOR

Lex Luthor is a rich businessman who tries to control Metropolis. Superman knows Lex isn't the good guy he claims to be. He has to take Lex down—fast!

The "S" symbol on Superman's chest is not just his initial. It is also the crest of his Kryptonian family, the House of El.

Superman

Need a snack? I don't ... I get my energy from **SOLAR POWER!**

I can fly four times **FASTER** THAN SOUND

I'll fire my **HEAT VISION** to melt your suit, Lex!

FIRESTORM VS. FIREFLY

That pesky Firefly is starting fires everywhere just for fun. But Firestorm, the nuclear hero, is in hot pursuit. This battle could be explosive!

Firestorm can manipulate nuclear energy. He uses it to fly, transform objects, and fire explosive energy blasts!

I'M ABOUT TO GO NUCLEAR ...

I'll tweak the **ATOMS** in your blaster and turn it into a sticky bun!

Firestorm

DID YOU KNOW?

Firestorm is two people in one! Scientist Jason Rusch and sporty Ronnie Raymond were joined together by the "Firestorm Matrix."

MERA vs. BLACK MANTA

A shark is chasing Black Manta and Mera! Who is most likely to escape: Black Manta with his technology or Mera with her Atlantean powers?

Queen Mera of Atlantis is a super-fast swimmer. She often travels at 300,000 miles an hour—and that's just her cruising speed!

I'M NOBODY'S FAST FOOD!

Mera

DID YOU KNOW?

Mera controls water with just her thoughts. She can build solid objects out of water or use it to create powerful blasts.

Back off, or I'll **BLAST** you both out of the water!

LEX ON THE LOOSE

Billionaire Lex Luthor is stomping in his mech while The Cheetah steals the Energy Infuser. The Super Heroes must stop them!

I'LL DODGE YOUR BULKY MECH!

Lex has great technology, but **BATMAN'S GADGETS** are top of the line!

DID YOU KNOW?

Lex's mech has a Kryptonite prison at the back. Lex's archenemy Superman is trapped inside. Oh no!

Mech has flexible hands to grasp Super Heroes!

Maybe Wonder Woman's lasso can grab back the Energy Infuser

Energy Infuser

I'LL KNOCK SPOTS OFF YOU!

Rotating stud shooter cannon

The mech's cockpit doubles as an escape pod. If Lex presses the eject button, it will detach so that he can make a speedy getaway.

Energy blasts

Look out for these STOMPING FEET!

SHAZAM vs. PARADEMON

Argh! The tyrant Darkseid has sent one of his Parademons to ravage the Earth. Can Shazam send the invader packing—without his stolen loot?

Billy Batson is a teenage boy, but if he says "Shazam!", he becomes a superpowered hero. A wizard gave him his amazing abilities.

GIVE THAT BACK, YOU PESKY PARADEMON!

Stand back! This blue bolt of **ENERGY** means I'm powering up ...

I have the powers of the legendary **GREEK GODS**

Shazam

DID YOU KNOW?

Blue Beetle is allowed to borrow the Batcopter to chase after Killer Moth. Batman trusts his beetle buddy to fly carefully!

YOU'RE JUST A PEST. ADIOS!

My armor is **ROBOTIC** and loaded with weapons

Blue Beetle

If things get tight, I'll call my teammates: **THE TEEN TITANS**

I'll open a **WORMHOLE** in space ... and send you through it!

All my shots are **RIGHT ON TARGET**

My jet pack allows me to make a **QUICK EXIT** when I need to!

Deadshot

Wielding this **GIANT BAZOOKA** takes real strength

Who will leave his enemy on the scrap heap?

OR

STEALTH is my game ... I just appear out of nowhere!

HA! CAUGHT YOU OFF GUARD!

Katana

I was trained by **TADASHI,** the famous samurai. Beat that!

Nobody sees me without my **MASK!**

KATANA VS. TALON

Who is the finest ninja fighter? Heroic Katana and a villainous Talon plan to settle the matter. Expect amazing swordplay and sneaky skills!

Katana excels at martial arts and hand-to-hand combat. Her sword, the Soultaker, is very old. It was forged back in the 1300s.

I hide out in the **TUNNELS** under the city.

TWO SWORDS ARE BETTER THAN ONE!

DID YOU KNOW?

The Talons are trained assassins who work for criminals called the Court of Owls. They are known as Talons because of their bladed claws.

ELECTRUM implants give me healing powers

Talon

Who is the nimblest ninja in Gotham City?

 OR

My amazing **ELECTRONIC EYE** gives me superhuman vision

If only you had ears, I'd stun you with my **SOUND AMPLIFIER**

I SEE YOU, OMAC. BOOYAH!

Cyborg

CYBORG VS. OMAC

When machines don't see eye-to-eye, expect a serious clash! Cyborg must stop OMAC from leading a cyber army invasion. Can he do it?

After a bad accident, half of Cyborg's body was rebuilt with robotic parts. Now he is half man, half machine—and all hero!

96

I can fire mighty **POWER BLASTS** from my eye and hands. Prepare to be dazzled!

YOU'LL SOON BE SEEING DOUBLE!

©LEGO

DID YOU KNOW?

OMAC is a member of a large cybernetic army controlled by a sinister satellite orbiting the Earth. The satellite's name is Brother Eye.

OMAC

I'm infected with a **HIGH-TECH VIRUS ...** I couldn't stop if I wanted to!

Which machine will overpower his foe?

OR

Lex Luthor is a rich, corrupt businessman in Metropolis. He loathes the *Daily Planet*, as it supports his archenemy, Superman.

LOIS LANE VS. LEX LUTHOR

Lex Luthor has been desperately trying to extract information out of reporter Lois Lane. He's tried bribery, tricks, and bugging. Now it's time to battle!

HURRY UP ... I'M DUE AT THE BARBER'S!

Tell me Superman's identity or I'll **BLAST** your camera!

Lex Luthor

I'll get the Daily Planet **BANNED!**

Who will survive with their reputation intact?

WONDER WOMAN VS. KILLER FROST

Killer Frost wants to turn the Amazons' homeland, Themyscira, into an icy waste. Wonder Woman won't have that. She's about to bring the heat of battle!

Wonder Woman has a bird design on her shield. It's the symbol of her people, warrior women called the Amazons.

My magic **BRACELETS** stop missiles (even icy ones)!

Wonder Woman

I could keep fighting forever thanks to my awesome **STAMINA**

CHAPTER 4: LOYAL FRIENDS

Super Heroes and super-villains are tough, but they can't go it alone all the time. Luckily, they have friends and allies like Robin and Krypto to help them on their missions.

GORDON VS. HENCHMEN

Some LexCorp workers are loading illegal Kryptonite at the docks. Commissioner Gordon is chasing them down—but will they come quietly?

Commissioner Gordon can handle most crimes alone, but if things get dicey, he uses the Bat-Signal to call Batman.

STOP ... THAT'S ILLEGAL!

GCPD

POLICE

Police car

I've spent **20 YEARS** fighting crime!

I'm used to combat ... I was in the **US MILITARY**

There's enough **KRYPTONITE** here to knock out Superman!

WE'RE JUST DOING OUR JOB!

Look out ... our truck has **MISSILE** launchers

LexCorp forklift

Who will get possession of the shady goods?

OR

DID YOU KNOW?

Rā's al Ghūl's hideout contains sneaky traps, like the swinging axe at the bottom of these stairs. Look out, Robin!

MY HOOD
shields my ears from sand ... and from your screeches!

If I have to, I'll use this staff to **POLE VAULT** out of reach!

Robin

ROBIN VS. TALIA AL GHŪL

Talia is loyal to her dad but also admires his enemy, Batman. She is a bit jealous of Robin because he is Batman's sidekick!

Rā's al Ghūl has asked his daughter, Talia, to capture Robin. She's really going for it! It's the Bat-Family against the al Ghūl family, but who will win?

I'll **SLICE** your staff into **SPLINTERS!**

My name means "Daughter of the **DEMON**"

WHY DON'T YOU BACKFLIP AWAY!

Talia al Ghūl

Which dueler will defeat their opponent?

A receiver in MY COLLAR lets me know when Batman needs me

TIME TO GET RUFF!

DID YOU KNOW?

Batman rescued Ace from the dog pound. He trained his new friend to fight crime and gave him his hood and collar.

Ace the Bat-Hound

ACE vs. CATWOMAN

Ace the Bat-Hound has cornered Catwoman in the middle of a jewel heist. Better step back—the fur is about to fly!

Ace has sharp teeth and a keen sense of smell. Like Batman, he wears a cape and cowl to hide his identity.

AIRLIFT ATTACK

Big, bad Steppenwolf and the Parademons are attacking! The Super Heroes arrive in their Flying Fox to stop him.

Superman is using his heat vision to turn the heat up on Steppenwolf

DID YOU KNOW?

This giant villain is from the planet Apokolips. Big bones must run in the family—he is the uncle of enormous bad guy Darkseid.

WHY DON'T YOU PICK ON SOMEONE YOUR OWN SIZE?

Steppenwolf's **HUGE AXE** is no match for Wonder Woman's shield

ROBIN VS. THE PENGUIN

Batman is away, so the Penguin has decided to attack his sidekick, Robin. The Boy Wonder must try to defeat the sneaky, beaky villain all on his own!

Robin has been training with Batman since the age of 8. He is now an expert in martial arts and cunning disguises.

Robin

TIME TO CAGE YOU, PENGUIN!

Only a **TEENAGE HERO** could rock this classic costume!

Ha! I'll run circles around you with my **ACROBATIC ABILITIES!**

The Penguin

I've got weapons hidden **IN MY UMBRELLA!**

I'M TOO CLEVER FOR YOU, BIRDBRAIN!

DID YOU KNOW?

There is a lie detector in the Batcave. The Penguin plans to wire Robin up to it and ask him where Batman is. A fib will make the red light glow!

Money squawks! This expensive **TUXEDO AND TOP HAT** turn my waddle into a swagger!

Who will win this battle of the birds?

OR

KRYPTO VS. LOBO

That mean old bounty hunter Lobo has come after Krypto, Superman's dog. Fur will fly and snarls will echo through space. Who will end up as top dog?

MY FREEZE BREATH will make you look even cooler!

Your Spacehog can't beat a **FLYING DOG**

I'll fetch *you* and take you back to **SUPERMAN**

Krypto

Lobo is from the planet Czarnia. He likes to look cool and tough! He wears black leather biker gear with chains and scary skulls.

HERE'S A DEADLY POWER BURST. FETCH!

DID YOU KNOW?

Lobo travels the galaxy hunting Super Heroes. He rides a bike called the Spacehog. He can speak many alien languages.

Lobo

I used my amazing **SENSE OF SMELL** to track you down from across the galaxy.

Which one will make his foe flee?

OR

IS THAT A COWL ON THE COAT RACK?

There's nobody as agile as me ... I always **LAND ON MY FEET!**

Nice suit, but my sleek black **CATSUIT** is more chic!

Catwoman

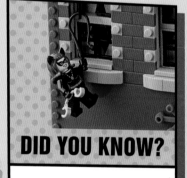

DID YOU KNOW?

Catwoman can easily break into tall buildings. She uses her claws to climb walls and her whip to pull open windows.

Who will win the Wayne Manor stand-off?

OR

THE JOKER WINS!

If you think the Joker and his wicked super-villain pals won more of their battles, choose this villainous victory.

TAKE THAT, SUPER HEROES!

The Joker and his buddies have used their tricks to beat the Super Heroes. The Joker can't stop grinning!

SUPER-VILLAINS RULE!

INDEX

Editor Rosie Peet
Project Art Editor Sam Bartlett
Designer Thelma Jane Robb
US Editor Kayla Dugger
Senior Production Editor Jennifer Murray
Senior Production Controller Lloyd Robertson
Managing Editor Paula Regan
Managing Art Editor Jo Connor
Art Director Lisa Lanzarini
Publisher Julie Ferris
Publishing Director Mark Searle

Dorling Kindersley would like to thank Randi Sørensen, Heidi K. Jensen,
Paul Hansford, and Martin Leighton Lindhardt at the LEGO Group;
Stefan Georgiou at DK for design assistance;
and Sadie Smith for proofreading.

First American Edition, 2020
Published in the United States by DK Publishing
1450 Broadway, Suite 801, New York, NY 10018

Page design copyright © 2020 Dorling Kindersley Limited
20 21 22 23 24 10 9 8 7 6 5 4 3 2 1
001–316399–Aug/2020

Manufactured by Dorling Kindersley 80 Strand, London, WC2R 0RL
under licence from the LEGO Group.

A catalog record for this book is available
from the Library of Congress.

ISBN: 978-1-4654-9239-5
978-0-7440-2145-5 (library edition)

Printed and bound in China

For the curious

www.LEGO.com
www.dk.com